THE NEW ADVENTURES OF MR TOAD

A Race for Toad Hall

Tom Moorhouse
with pictures by Holly Swain

OXFORD
UNIVERSITY PRESS

Contents

The Illustrious Heritage of Toad of Toad Hall

(and certain of His Friends and Foes)

Compiled by Toad in the year 2016

with special notes from Teejay

Toad of Toad Hall

Son of Old Mr Toad. Handsome and brave. Noble and kind. Excellent singing voice. ~~Best~~ worst driver in the whole world. NOT Very modest. Proud owner of Toad Hall. Spent a century frozen in his own ice house[1]. *still needs fixing* Rescued by really, really brave children (see below). His hair has turned white, — *and he's a bit wrinkly* but he is quite as dashing as he ever was.

He snores!

Toad Junior or 'Teejay'[2]

I'm not an egg!

Fine young Toad, all-round good egg. Parents travelling abroad (lucky fellows!). Lives with one 'Ms Badger' (a ~~fearsome~~ lady).
very nice

Ms Badger

I don't know what WW is. We live in a house.

Presume related to Mr Badger, but no longer living in WW. Guardian of Teejay. Completely ~~terrifying~~.
lovely

Don't be rude

Badge is looking after me for Mum and Dad

footnotes

is Mr T part of my family?

[1] Dratted stoats.
[2] I believe the family to be descended from my second cousin, old 'Toastie' Toad St John.

I ate a toastie last week

7

Ratty

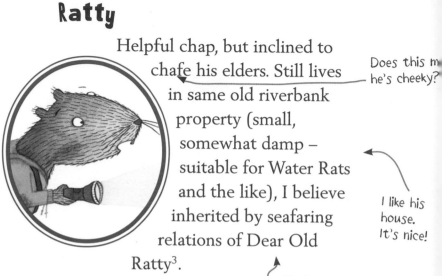

Helpful chap, but inclined to chafe his elders. Still lives in same old riverbank property (small, somewhat damp – suitable for Water Rats and the like), I believe inherited by seafaring relations of Dear Old Ratty[3].

Does this m[ean] he's cheeky?

I like his house. It's nice!

Badge says Ratty's granddad was a sailor

MO

Quiet sort. Good with those ~~Dumb Pewter~~ computer things. A Mole through and through – can tell just looking at him. Great, great grandson-mole (or what-have-you) of my Moly.

because he IS a mole, silly!

Mr T's friend from the photo

8

Chief Executive Weasel

he's horrid

Nasty fellow. Small paws, shifty eyes. Most likely related to the Old Chief Weasel[4].

Mr Ripton

Very thin and grey. Weasel lackey.

↑

what's a lackey?

footnotes

[3] Got this from a field-mouse. Check accuracy.

[4] Unmitigated scoundrel! ← and other words Mr T says, like bounder and cad. And ne'er-do-well. And blighter and rotter. (He says I'm a flibbertigibbet.)

9

Chapter 1
Mole in a Hole

Teejay peeked out from the bush she was hiding in. She saw Ratty first, coming up from the river. The brown fur on his face and paws made him hard to spot. Only his jeans and hoodie gave him away.

'Over here,' hissed Teejay, waving. Ratty joined her with a rustle.

'I couldn't find you,' he said. 'You match the bush.'

Teejay grinned. 'Toads are good at hiding. And I wore my green t-shirt. Any trouble?'

'No, I told Mum I was going to your house.'

'Brilliant. Where's Mo?'

Ratty glanced around. 'Dunno. Maybe he's being *really* stealthy.'

From down towards Toad Hall came a crashing sound. A voice cried, 'Oh, I hate all these brambles.'

'Or maybe he isn't.'

And there was Mo, stomping up the hill. Teejay sighed. So much for being stealthy. But it wasn't really Mo's fault. He was a mole, and found everything outside too bright.

She waved him over. 'Did you keep it secret?' Teejay whispered.

Mo nodded. 'Dad thinks I'm at Rat's house.'

'Great. Right.' Teejay put on her best telling-people-what-to-do voice. 'Attention troops: today is mission "rope-swing". At the top of this hill is the rope Rat found yesterday.' Ratty gave a small bow. 'And today we're going to swing on it. Any questions?'

'Yes,' said Mo. 'Is it safe?'

'Oh, come on.'

12

Teejay led them to the top of the hill, where a rope hung from the tallest tree. She ran up and pulled it. The rope stretched, and something went *ping*.

'See? It's fine.'

'I don't think—' Mo began, but Teejay had been waiting all day for this.

'Stand back!' she cried. And she launched.

The world tilted as the swing carried her up high. All of Toad Hall's grounds spread below her. She saw the river and trees, and the crumbled walls and broken windows of Toad Hall itself. And then she was racing back towards Mo and Ratty.

'Out of the way, out of the way!' Teejay's legs dragged in the grass. She fell over backwards.

'How was it?' said Ratty.

'That,' said Teejay, 'was amazing.' She got up, and handed Ratty the rope. 'Your turn.'

Ratty held on tight and jumped. Teejay giggled at his tail, streaming out behind him. As he swung back, the rope went **twaaaang.** Ratty landed, grinning, and gave Mo the rope.

'Give it a go, Mo!'

Mo looked like he would rather be holding a snake. He tugged the rope. It went **doii-iing.** 'Yikes! I don't think it's strong enough.'

'Scaredy-mole.'

Mo pushed his glasses up his nose. 'Am not.' He closed his eyes. 'Oh,' he whimpered. 'Oh noooooooooooo!'

He swung out like a tubby conker.
The rope **tightened** . . .

The rope **strained** . . .

The rope
creaked . . .

It snapped.

Mo!

Mo dropped through the
bushes. Teejay heard a yell and
a thud. She and Ratty raced
down the slope, shouting Mo's
name. But at the bottom there
was no sign of him.

'Look, there!' said Ratty. He
pointed at a new, Mo-sized
hole in the ground.

Teejay ran up to the edge.
'Mo, are you in there?'

'Yes. I—I *told* you it wasn't
safe.'

Teejay sagged with relief.

'Phew! He's
OK. Shine your
torch down, Rat.'
Ratty pulled
out a torch. In its
light Mo blinked up
at them. 'Get me out of
here!'

He still had his glasses
on. But he was a very long
way down.

'Right,' said Teejay. 'Erm,
how?'

'I'm still holding my bit of rope.'

'Great thinking, Mo! Throw it up
and we'll pull you out.'

But it was tricky. Teejay and Ratty
leaned right in but couldn't catch the rope.

'It's no good. We have to get closer.' They crawled forwards until their heads were over the hole. Mo threw again. The rope *just* slipped through Teejay's fingers.

'Argh. Nearly.' She crept further out. 'Try again, Mo!'

Mo frowned. He pulled back his arm and threw. And Teejay grabbed the rope.

'Yes!'

But then the ground shifted. Teejay grabbed at grass, soil, anything—but too late. The earth gave way, and she and Ratty tumbled down into soil-scented darkness.

Chapter 2
Terrible Tunnels

'**Y**ou were meant to pull me out,' said Mo, 'not fall down here too.'

'Huh,' said Teejay.

Ratty was searching for his torch. 'Got it!' He turned it on. He pulled a face. 'We'll never climb out. The soil's all crumbly. Let's shout for help.'

'But no one ever comes to Toad Hall,' said Teejay. 'We're really stuck.'

Mo, though, was on his feet. 'No we're not. Look at that!'

He ran to the wall and began to dig. Soil

flew from Mo's paws, and soon he was standing in front of a neat, round opening, just shorter than he was.

'See? See? We're not in a hole. We're in a *tunnel*. It got filled with mud when I fell in.'

'Clever Mo!' said Teejay. 'That means there's a way out.'

'Maybe,' said Mo with a frown. 'But what if the other end's blocked?'

'Well, it's better than sitting here,' Teejay

decided. 'Let's explore. You go first, Mo, because you're best at tunnels.'

Mo set off, sniffing the air and muttering to himself. He moved so quickly that Teejay had to run to keep up. Soon the daylight was gone. It could have been scary without

Ratty's torch, but Teejay was enjoying herself. This was a proper adventure.

'Um, Teejay?' Ratty sounded nervous.

'Yes?'

'Does this go to Toad Hall?'

Mo stopped dead. Teejay nearly ran into the back of him. 'Oh, no,' Mo quavered. 'Not Toad Hall. Not with the ghost!'

'What ghost?' Teejay scoffed.

'Old Mr Toad,' whispered Ratty. 'He haunts the house.'

Mr Toad had vanished a hundred years ago, and Toad Hall had been empty ever since.

'He's not haunting, he went travelling,' said Teejay. 'Like Mum and Dad when I was little. It's a Toad thing.'

But Mo shook his head. 'That's what the weasels told everyone,' he whispered. 'But people say he's still here, somewhere in the Hall.'

Even Teejay felt a shiver. But ghost or no ghost they had to get out of this tunnel.

'Right. Stop being silly, you two,' said Teejay. 'There's no such thing as ghosts. Keep going, Mo.'

She poked Mo until he set off. He ran ahead and around a bend. There was a thud and a yelp.

'Owdth! I bagged by bose.'

'You bagged your bose?' said Teejay. 'Oh, you banged your nose. Poor Mo!'

'Yedth. And the tunnelth blogged off.'

Blocked off? Teejay joined Mo. She reached out for the walls and roof. Instead of mud they were dry, and rough to touch.

'Strange. This feels like wood.'

Mo let go of his nose, and tapped the wall in front of him.

'So does this,' he said. 'And there's something else. Oh!'

Ratty squeezed in and held up his torch. Its light showed Mo, pointing at a round, shiny object.

'I think it's a doorknob,' said Mo.

Chapter 3
The Toad Hall Ghost

The tunnel ended at a little yellow door with a brass doorknob. The door was covered in dirt and cobwebs. Mo wiped it with his sleeve.

'Look. Writing.'

On the door were the words *Mr Toad's Ice House*, neatly painted. Below them someone else had written *Frozed Tode: Keep Shut*.

'What's an "Ice House"?' said Ratty.

'And what's a "Frozed Tode"?' asked Teejay. She reached for the doorknob. But Ratty grabbed her arm.

'Wait! Listen!'

A moan rose out of the air.

Snnnnnaaaaaaaaa. Snnnnnaaaaaaaaa.

'It's the ghost,' cried Mo.

Snnnnnaaaaaaaaa. Snnnnnaaaaaaaaa.

'A ghost, a ghost,' Mo whimpered. 'It's going to get us!'

But Teejay started to giggle. 'It's not a ghost, silly,' she said. 'It's snoring. Ghosts don't snore.'

Ratty's whiskers twitched. 'Phew! Let's see who's in there,' he said. 'Maybe they can help us.'

'Good idea, Rat,' said Teejay.

She grabbed the doorknob, twisted, and pulled. Something hissed and rushed out, cold over her feet.

'Argh!' Teejay scuttled away. In the torchlight the floor sparkled. 'It's ice,' Teejay gasped. 'It fell through the door.'

The room on the other side of the door was filled with ice, right up to the ceiling.

SNNNNNAAAAAAAAA. SNNNNNAAAAAAAAA.

'The snoring's coming from the back,' Ratty

whispered. 'Someone's in the ice!'

'But it's f-freezing,' said Mo. 'We have to get them out!'

'Right.' Teejay started digging. With Mo's help she soon cleared enough space to climb over the top.

'Rat, bring the torch,' Teejay ordered. 'Mo, you stand guard.'

Mo trembled. 'What do I do if I see something?'

'Squeak in fear.'

Then Teejay climbed up and Ratty followed. Together they slithered down the other side of the ice heap.

They stood, blinking.

'Wow,' said Ratty. 'That's weird.'

In front of them was a rough bed, badly made out of planks. It was almost buried in the ice. On it lay an old toad, fast asleep. His skin was pale and his hair was white. He wore an old–fashioned nightshirt and cap. He had a grey moustache, which fluttered as he snored.

SNNNNNAAAAAAAAA. SNNNNNAAAAAAAAA.

Teejay carefully touched his skin. 'Cold. Like an ice lolly.'

'But who wants a toad-flavoured ice lolly?' said Ratty.

Teejay shook the old toad's shoulder. 'Come on, wake up.'

SNNNNNAAAAAAAAA. SNNNNNAAAAAAAAA.

Ratty had a go. 'Wakey, wakey!' he yelled. 'Shake a leg! Rise and shine!'

SNNNNNAAAAAAAAA. SNNNNNAAAAAAAAA.

'Hmmm. Hang on.' Ratty pulled a balloon from his pocket. He blew it up and held it next to the toad's head. 'This should be good!'

The toad sat bolt upright, eyes swivelling. 'How bad was it? How bad was it?' he shouted. 'Did anyone see what I did?' A silly grin spread across his face. 'Ah, but wasn't she a beauty? Eh? **Poop-poop**!'

And then, very slowly, he fell backwards in a dead faint.

Chapter 4   Jam in the Pantry

'**O**ne, two, three ... heave!'

Teejay pushed while Mo and Ratty pulled on the toad's legs. Another shove got him right to the top of the ice heap.

'Good work,' Teejay panted. 'Now for the easy bit. Ready? One, two, three ...'

'No, wait—,' said Mo.

'Heave!' shouted Teejay, and pushed. The toad shot down the ice like a sledge and slid out into the tunnel. There was a loud **thud**, then a **sproink** and a long **creeaaak**.

'Oops,' said Teejay. They ran to the passage

to find the toad lying crumpled against a wall. 'Is he OK?'

One of the toad's eyes cracked open. 'Haha!' he said. 'Vroom!' Then he started snoring again.

'Depends what you mean by "OK",' said Ratty.

'Ooh, ooh, look!' said Mo.

Above their heads, where there had been a roof, was now a square hole. It was just big enough to squeeze through. Teejay could see up into what looked like a pantry, lined with shelves and plates.

'Brilliant, it's a trapdoor!' she said. 'I think it opened when he hit the wall.' She beamed at Ratty and Mo. 'I found the way out!'

'No you didn't,' said Ratty. 'You pushed a toad down some ice.'

'Doesn't matter.' Teejay's eyes were shining. 'That's Toad Hall up there. Let's go!'

Teejay climbed up first, then helped Ratty and Mo.

'See, we're saved. We just need a door.'

'One problem,' said Mo. 'How do we get *him* up here?'

Teejay peered down at the toad. He was out of reach. And he looked heavy.

'Good question.'

'We can use that,' said Ratty, pointing at a hook in the ceiling. He pulled out some rope, and grinned. 'It's Mo's bit from the swing.'

Ratty went down and tied the rope under the toad's arms. ('**SNNNNNAAAAAAAAA**' said the toad.) Then he climbed back up and threw it over the hook.

'Ta daa!'

'What happens now?' said Teejay

'We pull down, the toad comes up,' said Ratty. 'Easy.'

'Rat, you're a star.' Teejay took hold of the rope. 'Everyone ready? Then one, two, three, heave!'

The toad's feet came off the floor.

'Heave!'

His head and shoulders came up through the hole.

'Heave!'

The toad jammed tight, right around his middle.

'He's stuck!' shouted Ratty.

'Keep pulling,' ordered Teejay. 'One, two, three, heave!'

The toad did not move.

'Again, as hard as you can! Heave!'

And the toad popped out of the hole, landing on his bottom in front of them. His eyes blinked open.

'There's no need for roughness, officers,' he said. 'I wasn't even driving. It was an old washerwoman. Hahaha!' Then he whispered, 'Clever old Toady,' and fell asleep.

Ratty shook his head. 'He's not right, is he?'

'He's still really cold,' said Mo. 'We should warm him up.'

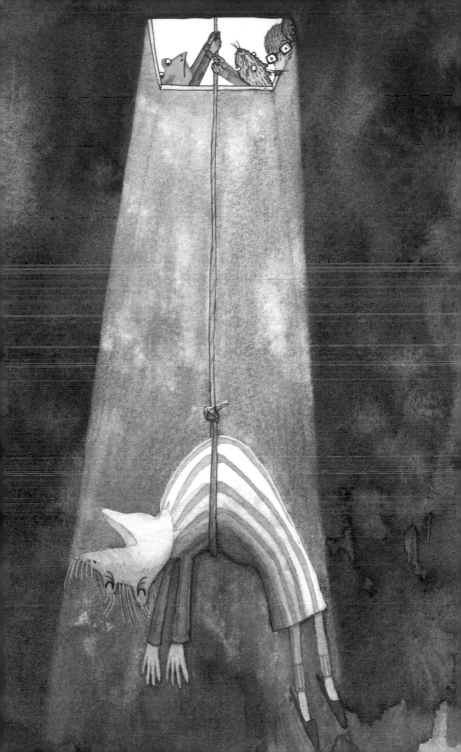

'Good idea, Mo,' said Teejay. 'Let's try to find some blankets.'

They raced off to explore the house. The pantry opened into a dining hall, then a maze of corridors and empty rooms. Everything was dark, echoey, and covered with dust.

HANDLE WITH CARE

They came out in a hallway. It was high, with an enormous front door and a wide staircase.

'Oh look, big dangly light things,' said Ratty.

'They're chandeliers,' said Mo. 'But have a look at these pictures!'

'Never mind those, that's the way up,' said Teejay. 'Come on!'

Together they dashed up to the bedrooms, searching in chests and boxes. Ratty opened a wardrobe. 'Aha!'

He came out with a heap of blankets. 'There were clothes too,' said Ratty. 'Lots of old suits and stuff.'

'Great,' said Teejay. 'Let's warm up our toad!'

But when they got back to the pantry it was empty. The rope lay coiled on the floor.

And the toad had vanished.

Chapter 5
Signs at the Door

'**W**here did he go?' said Teejay. 'We need to find him, we—'

A hammering sound rang through the house. They froze.

'What's that?' Mo squeaked.

'Sounds like the front door,' said Ratty. 'But nobody lives here.'

'Maybe someone *is* looking for us,' said Teejay.

More hammering, even louder.

'What are we going to do?' whispered Mo. 'I don't want to get into trouble.'

'Ignore it,' Teejay whispered. 'They'll go away.'

But then she heard the sound of a key rattling in a lock. And bolts scraped back, first one then another. Teejay sprinted for the hall, the others just behind. She got there in time to see the old toad, holding the door handle.

'Humph. Must be the butler's day off,' he said, and pulled the door wide.

He put his hands on his hips.

'I say! You there!' he shouted. 'You two weaselly fellows, what do you think you're doing?'

Two weasels stood on the doorstep. One held a hammer and nails, and the other a sign bigger than he was. They stared at the toad. The hammer fell from the first weasel's grip. (It clunked to the ground, just missing his toes.) He nudged the other weasel.

'Wesley,' he whispered, 'Wesley, that's him.'

'Him who, Wilbur?'

'*Him*. You know . . . *him*. The toad.'

'What, him? Don't be daft. He's all frozen up.'

'Shhhh!' hissed the first weasel.

The toad glared at the pair of them. He grabbed the sign, held it up, and read it aloud:

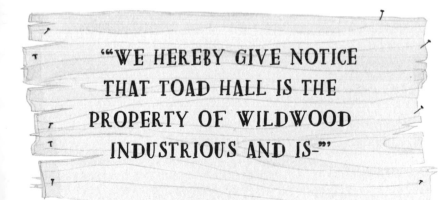

"WE HEREBY GIVE NOTICE THAT TOAD HALL IS THE PROPERTY OF WILDWOOD INDUSTRIOUS AND IS—"

He stopped dead.

'*Property*? My lovely Toad Hall? Someone else's property? I don't think so!' He stuck out his chest and walked up to the nearest weasel. 'And what would you scoundrels do with my home? More weasel dinner parties, I expect? More drinking my wine? More singing songs about how silly I am? Eh?'

The weasels exchanged looks. 'Um, no. We're knocking it down, matey.'

'Knocking it down?' The toad goggled at him. '*Knocking it down?*' he shrieked. 'I'll show you who's getting knocked down!'

And he hit the first weasel right on the head with the sign.

Smack!

'Ouch!'

The weasel rubbed his ear. The other held up his paws, 'Now look, mate—' he began, but the toad hit him too.

Whack!

46

'Ow! You can't—'

Thump!

'I certainly can. Take that, you rotten weasel!'

Clout!

'Ooh!' The weasels started backing away. 'Come on, there's no need to—'

Thwack! Wallop!

And the weasels ran for it. The toad chased them down the drive, nightshirt flapping. He kept hitting each of them in turn until they fled through the gate.

'Impudent young scamps!'

The toad dropped the sign—which now had weasel-sized holes in it—dusted his hands and turned back to Toad Hall.

But when he saw its broken roof and the ivy growing through the walls his eyes widened. His bottom lip started to shake.

'B-b-but it's ruined!' A tear trickled down his cheek. 'It didn't look like this when I went to bed!'

And he fell to his knees and began to cry.

Chapter 6
Mr Toad Himself

Teejay rushed to the toad's side.

'Oh, don't cry. It'll be all right,' she said. 'It will, won't it, Mo?'

'I don't know,' Mo frowned. 'There *is* quite a lot of damage.'

The toad sobbed louder.

'It'll be fine,' said Ratty, quickly.

The toad sniffed and looked up. 'Do you really think so?'

'Of course,' said Ratty. 'It just needs . . .' He paused. 'Well, completely rebuilding, actually.'

The toad rolled on the ground, wailing.

Teejay glared at Mo and Ratty. Then she heard a crunch of gravel. She turned to see a car coming down the drive.

'Uh oh,' Ratty whispered. 'Isn't that Ms Badger's car?'

'Yep, that's Badge,' Teejay gulped. She looked down at her ripped jacket and filthy leggings. Ratty and Mo too were covered in mud and scratches. 'Well, it's been nice knowing you both. Once Badge sees us she won't ever let me out again.'

Ms Badger stopped the car, and got out. Then she ran up and pulled Teejay into a hug.

'Toad Junior, what on earth have you been up to? I've been worried sick!'

Teejay hung her head. 'Um, we had an accident.'

'An accident? Are you OK?'

Teejay nodded. Ms Badger put a paw over her eyes. 'Oh, why me? They never said being your guardian would be *this* much trouble.' But she smiled, and squeezed Teejay tight.

'I'm really sorry, Badge,' said Teejay. 'How did you find us?'

'Hah! You're *always* hanging around Toad Hall.' Ms Badger folded her arms. 'And didn't I tell you not to come to here?'

At the sound of the engine the toad had stopped crying and climbed to his feet. His fingers twitched, as if holding a steering wheel. He finally took his eyes from Ms Badger's car, and stepped forwards.

'Dear lady, please don't be angry,' he said. 'I may be a little out of sorts, but I'm certain these wonderful children have saved me from some villainous weasel plot.'

Ms Badger blinked. 'Excuse me,' she said, 'but who exactly are you?'

The toad smiled. 'Of course, you must be new to these parts. Everyone who's anyone knows *me*. But permit me to introduce myself.' He swept a hand at Toad Hall. 'I am the dashing proprietor of this most magnificent of hereditary establishments.'

'What does that mean?' Teejay hissed to Mo.

'He owns Toad Hall,' Mo whispered back.

'In short, madam, standing before you is none other than Mr Toad himself!'

Mr Toad bowed low to Ms Badger.

She raised an eyebrow. 'I have two questions. First, where are your clothes?'

Mr Toad looked down at his nightshirt. His mouth dropped open.

'There are some inside,' said Teejay.

'And second,' Ms Badger continued, 'do you really live there?'

Mr Toad looked back at the ruined house. His shoulders slumped. 'I used to. I'm not certain that I can any more.'

'Right,' said Ms Badger. 'Well, I'm going to take this lot home and get them cleaned up. You'd better get dressed and come along. She frowned at Teejay. 'And then, I think, *somebody* will have quite a lot of explaining to do.'

Chapter 7
Windipedia

'**I**t's definitely him,' said Mo.

Teejay peered at the laptop on Ms Badger's table. It showed a black and white picture of a toad, standing in front of Toad Hall. She glanced at Mr Toad, who was pushing all the buttons on the coffee machine and waving his cup at it. He looked exactly the same, even the suit and shoes, only older, and now his hair was white. But Toad Hall was completely different. In the picture it was all neat and trim.

'Where did you find the photo?' said Ms Badger.

'It's on Windipedia,' said Mo. 'I searched for Toad Hall, and there he was.'

Coffee whooshed onto the floor. Mr Toad jumped away, brushing his waistcoat. 'Dashed thing's broken,' he said. 'What are you chaps looking at?'

He shoved in between Ratty and Mo. 'Why, that's my photograph! However did it get in there?'

Mo grinned. He clicked on the photo so it filled the screen.

Mr Toad goggled. 'How did you do that? What is this thing?' He started to tap at the keyboard. Mo moved the laptop out of reach.

'It's a computer,' said Ratty.

'A Dumb Pewter?' Mr Toad's eyes were shining. 'Where do I get one?'

Ms Badger shook her head. 'It can't be him. That picture must be a century old.'

'Don't be silly,' scoffed Mr Toad. 'It was taken last April.'

Mo scrolled down and read the words below

the photograph. 'It says, "Toad of Toad Hall, 1916, shortly before his disappearance".'

'I didn't disappear. Look!' Mr Toad held up an arm and waved it up and down. Then he stopped. 'Why are you all staring at me like that?'

'Maybe you *did* disappear,' said Mo, slowly. 'We found you in the ice house . . . what if you've been in there all along?'

Teejay's mouth fell open. 'You mean he could really have been—'

'—frozen. For a hundred years,' finished Ratty. 'Wow.'

Mo scrolled down the webpage. 'Look at this!' he said.

The screen now showed a different photograph. In this one a group of animals were sitting with Mr Toad in a cosy front room.

'Hang on, that's my house,' said Ratty. 'We've still got that chair.'

'Oh my goodness.' Ms Badger pointed at the screen. 'Granddad Badger had this on his

wall. He said it was a photo of his father.'

'Did he say who the others were?' said Teejay.

Ms Badger shook her head. 'I was still just a cub when he died. I'm sorry, I don't know them.'

Mr Toad, though, was staring at the laptop, open-mouthed.

'I do,' he said in a tiny voice. 'I do.'

Chapter 8

Toad Acres

The room went quiet.

'Oh, my dear Ratty and Moly,' said Mr Toad. 'I only saw them last week. And poor, brave old Badger.' He looked up at Ms Badger. 'And now—' He hesitated. 'Now, do you think he's . . . gone?'

'I'm so, so sorry,' said Ms Badger. 'But yes, he must have. Many years ago.'

'I see.' Mr Toad took a breath. 'Tell me, might my good Moly and Ratty still be here?'

Ratty looked at Mo, then down at the floor. 'There's just me, Mum and Dad at home.'

And Mo shook his head. 'The photo's really old. He'd be my great, great grandmole.'

'Ah.' Mr Toad gazed at the table top. Then he pulled out a handkerchief and held it against his eyes while his shoulders shook. Ms Badger quietly set a cup of coffee down in front of him.

'All gone,' whispered Mr Toad. He took a sip of coffee, and closed his eyes. 'My wonderful friends, my poor Toad Hall. Oh, miserable Toad, what am I to do?'

Nobody knew what to say.

'We'll help you,' said Teejay, finally. 'We'll get your home fixed.' She looked at Ms Badger, Ratty, and Mo. 'That's right, isn't it?'

Everyone nodded.

PROPERTY
OF
MOLE

Mr Toad smiled up at them through his tears. 'Sweet children, dear lady,' he murmured. 'Thank you. Thank you.'

'Um, Ms Badger?' Ratty was looking at the laptop. 'There might be a problem with fixing Toad Hall.'

Right at the bottom of the Windipedia page were the words:

Please note: Toad Hall has recently been acquired by Wildwood Industrious.

Mo clicked on a link, and a new page came up. This one had a drawing of hundreds of houses, next to a giant sawmill on a bend in the river. Underneath it said: 'Wildwood Industrious proudly presents *Toad Acres*. Weasenably Priced and Stoatally Modern Houses. Live for Today, not for Toady. Badger Your Estate Agent for Details!'

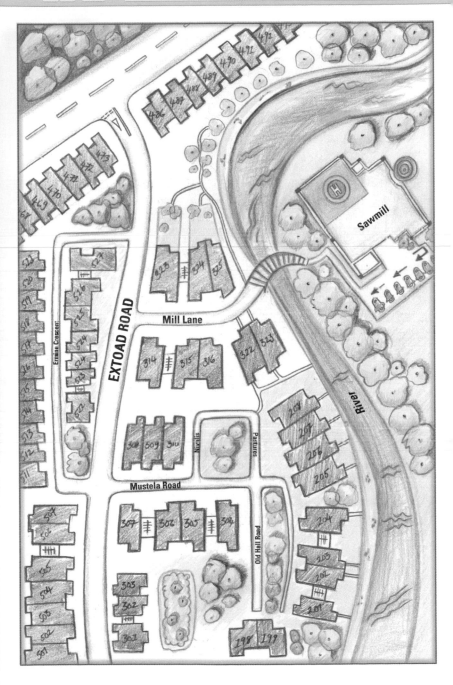

Mr Toad peered at the screen. 'Those are the grounds of Toad Hall, I'm sure of it. But where's my house gone?'

'Oh no!' said Mo. 'They really are going to knock it down.'

'And then they'll build all those houses,' said Ms Badger.

Mr Toad shot to his feet. 'Those despicable creatures! I'm not having it. They've gone too far! Too far, I tell you!'

He stared wildly about the room. He spied Ms Badger's car keys, grabbed them and ran to the door. He flung it open.

'Haha!' cried Mr Toad, one finger jabbing at the sky. 'The dastardly weasels reckoned without the righteous and indignant Toad. They want *Toad Acres*, do they? Well they'll all be achers when Toad is done with them!'

Then he leapt from the house and dashed for the car.

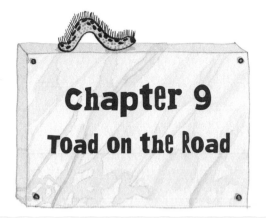

chapter 9
Toad on the Road

Teejay and Ratty got to the car just as Mr Toad started the engine.

'Wait,' shouted Teejay. 'Hang on.'

She opened the door and they climbed in.

'Don't try to stop me! I'll learn 'em!' cried Mr Toad. Then he hesitated. 'I say, where is this Wildweasel place?'

'It's Wildwood,' said Teejay. 'And we'll show you. Hurry up, Mo! Get in!'

'But . . .' Mo ran up, panting. 'But he doesn't have a driving licence.'

'Just get in, will you?'

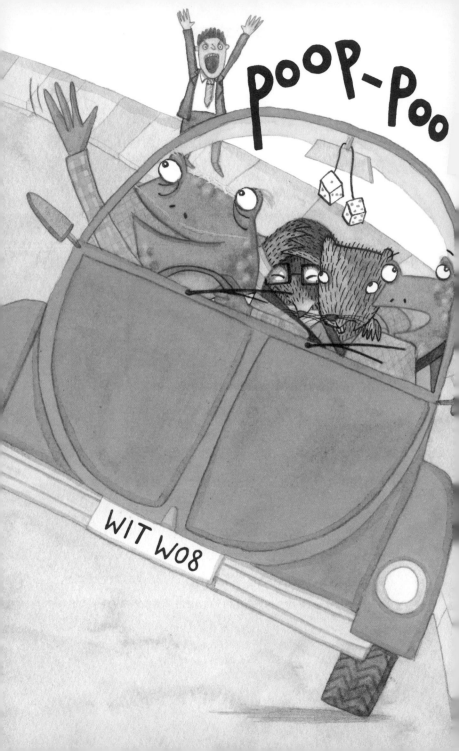

'But, but . . . Oh no!' said Mo, and jumped in the car.

'Away, away! We're off to whack the weasels!' shouted Mr Toad.

Mr Toad waggled levers and stamped on pedals. The engine roared. The car did not move. He waggled again and stamped even harder. And this time the car roared off.

'Wheee!' shouted Mr Toad. 'Where are the driving goggles?'

'Forget the goggles,' yelled Ratty. 'Put your seatbelt on!'

They flew around a bend. Teejay clicked her own seatbelt with one hand, holding on for dear life with the other.

'Turn left here,' she shouted.

The car went around the corner like a missile. It bumped over the pavement.

'Argh!' yelled Ratty. 'What are you doing?'

'Driving!' Mr Toad shouted. 'I'm the finest driver in the world!'

Mo put his head in his paws. 'We're going to crash,' he whimpered.

'Now turn right!' shouted Teejay.

The wheels left black marks on the road. Horns beeped, and people dived for safety. Mr Toad pressed the horn.

Poop-poop!

'**Poop-poop!**' whooped Mr Toad. 'Haha! Hear that, weasels?'

Poop-poop!

'**Poop-poop!** Toad will save the day!'

He swerved, just avoiding an accident.

'Watch where you're going!' Ratty shouted.

'Which way am I meant to be going?'

'Straight on!' yelled Teejay.

Mr Toad pressed harder on the pedal. The engine screamed. The car hurtled down the road.

'Here!' Teejay cried. 'Through that gate!'

Mr Toad spun the steering wheel. Teejay saw a sign saying *Wildwood Industrious* as it whipped past. Then the car smashed straight into a tree.

Crunch!

Everything went very quiet.

Mr Toad took his hands from the wheel.

'**Poopety-poop!**' he whispered. 'I never thought a car could go so *fast*.' Then he opened the door and jumped out.

'Poop is right,' said Ratty. 'That was really scary.'

'Fun, though,' said Teejay. 'Are you OK, Mo?'

Mo's head was still in his paws. 'I don't know. Have we stopped yet?'

Teejay helped Ratty and Mo out. They found Mr Toad staring at the crumpled front of the car.

'Some silly gardeners planted this tree in the way.'

'They didn't think you'd be driving on the lawn,' said Ratty.

'Never mind that,' said Mr Toad. 'Where's Weaselwood?'

'It's Wildwood,' said Mo. 'And it's there.'

Teejay turned Mr Toad so he was facing the

right way. In front of them was a huge glass office block. Weasels and stoats were at the windows, looking to see what the noise was.

'Aha! So they knew I was coming, did they?' said Mr Toad. 'Follow me!'

And he marched towards the front door.

wildwood
weaselwood
Industrious

chapter
10

A weasel in a suit met them at the door. 'Can I help?'

Mr Toad pushed straight past him. 'Stand aside. I'm here to see the Chief Weasel.'

'The Executive? Do you have an appointment?'

'I need no appointment. I am the wrathful Toad.'

'Who?'

But Mr Toad was gone. Teejay, Ratty, and Mo ran after him, past offices and desks. More stoats and weasels stopped to stare.

'Where's your Chief?' Mr Toad shouted and led the way up stairs and down corridors until they came to a door that said:

WILDWOOD INDUSTRIOUS

The Chief Executive Weasel

'Executive, eh? I'll give him an executing he'll never forget!'

Mr Toad flung open the doors. He marched right up to the Chief Weasel's desk. He thumped its shiny top.

'Now see here, you weasel,' he said. 'I don't like the way your fellows are eyeing up my home. Toad Hall belongs to me, so keep off or I'll call the law!' He turned to Teejay. 'That'll show him what's what.'

The Chief Weasel did not even blink. He pressed a button on his telephone. 'Could you send in Mr Ripton? Tell him that we have a "Code Green". Thank you.'

The Chief Weasel sat back. He folded his arms across the front of his suit.

'He doesn't look very worried,' whispered Ratty.

'He doesn't look surprised to see us, either,' said Mo.

A door opened and a tall, thin weasel came in. He had grey hair and wore a grey suit. He put a stack of paper on the desk then stood behind the Chief Weasel.

'Thank you, Mr Ripton,' said the Chief Weasel. He turned to Mr Toad. 'Now, what were you saying about Toad Hall?'

'I was saying that it's mine,'

85

said Mr Toad, 'and if you touch one brick of it I'll jolly well go to the police.'

'**Hurk, hurk**,' laughed the Chief Weasel. 'Hear that, Mr Ripton? He thinks he owns Toad Hall.'

Mr Ripton smiled.

'I do own it. I'm Toad of Toad Hall!'

'Not any more,' said the Chief Weasel. 'Now you're just "Toad". **Hurk hurk**.' He pushed the pile of paper across the desk. 'Do you know what this is?'

'It's paper.'

'Very good, Mr Toad, it *is* paper. But it's special paper with words on it, all written by Mr Ripton. He's my legal weasel.'

'I don't like the sound of this,' Mo whispered.

The Chief Weasel picked up the top sheet. 'The words say that Toad Hall belongs to me. It was empty for a hundred years, so we claimed it. All legal. Isn't that right, Mr Ripton?'

Mr Ripton nodded.

'So that's the way of it!' cried Mr Toad.

'Then let's see what your Mr Ripton thinks of this!'

He grabbed the paper, tore it up and threw it in the air.

'Toad Hall is mine! Mine, mine, mine!'

he shouted. 'How dare you claim it without asking me!'

He snatched more paper and screwed it into balls. He kicked it around the room and jumped up and down on it. Then he fell against the desk and started to cry.

'I didn't mean to leave Toad Hall empty,' sobbed Mr Toad. 'Why does everything have to be horrible?'

Chapter 11
The Challenge

The Chief Weasel watched it all with a smirk. 'Come, now, Mr Toad, it's not horrible,' he said. 'Once we've knocked your house down we'll build a sawmill. And then we'll use all those nasty damp trees in the Wild Wood to make lovely dry homes for our weasels.' He smiled. 'See? It'll be all new and shiny.'

Mr Toad's bottom lip trembled. 'How could you,' he whispered, and put his head in his arms.

'Deary me.' The Chief Weasel shook his head. 'You know, the old Chief used to call Mr

Toad "the scourge of the Wild Wood". Now look at him.' He turned to Mr Ripton. 'Do you think all that time in the ice house froze his brains? **Hurk hurk**.'

Mr Ripton's eyes widened. He waved his hands at the Chief Weasel. But too late.

Mo frowned. 'How do you know about the ice house? We only just found him in there.'

'That's right,' said Teejay. 'And who wrote "Frozed Tode" on the door?'

Ratty's jaw dropped open. 'What . . . you think *they* put him in the ice house?'

Mr Toad jumped to his feet.

'You rotters! You cads!' he shouted. 'You villainous Woodweasel scoundrels! I remember it all, now. Stoats in the night—they took me from my bed and locked me in my ice house.'

'That was their plan!' said Mo. 'Mr Toad had to be gone so they could claim Toad Hall.'

'And what are you going to do about it, Toady?' sneered the Chief Weasel. 'You can't prove anything. You're just a defrosted frog who's past his use-by date.'

'I'm going to challenge you, that's what!' cried Mr Toad. 'We'll settle this like gentlemen. I challenge you to a race with motor cars!' He waved a finger under the Chief Weasel's nose. 'If I win I get Toad Hall, if I don't it's yours. Unless you're a big weaselly chicken.'

The Chief Weasel's eyes narrowed.

He got up and walked to the window. He looked down at Ms Badger's car, and a toothy smile spread across his face.

91

'Will you be driving?'

'Of course! Find me your very best weasel and I'll beat him.'

'All right, Toady,' said the Chief Weasel, 'you have a deal.' He pulled out a calendar. 'Ah. Just two weeks till the Pipergate Races, Mr Ripton.'

Mr Ripton smiled, and nodded.

'Pipergate's famous,' said Mo to Mr Toad. 'It's a whole day of car races.'

Mr Toad's eyes shone. 'Then Pipergate it is! Which race?'

'You'll lose, so pick any,' sneered the Chief Weasel.

'Done!' cried Mr Toad. 'Get your Mr Ripton to write that down, and send it to my Mole, here. He'll tell you the race.' He winked at Teejay. 'All legal. Eh?'

He walked out of the office with his head up. But as Teejay followed she was sure she heard the Chief Weasel laughing.

Hurk, hurk, hurk.

Chapter 12
A Mole with a Plan

'**You** see, children, that's how you deal with weasels,' said Mr Toad, as they left. 'They'll be laughing on the other side of their pointy faces when I win that race.' He went up to Ms Badger's car. 'Maybe I can even use this fine vehicle.'

He patted the car. It hissed and the bumper fell off.

'Mr Toad,' said Teejay. 'Do you think the challenge was a *good* idea?'

'But of course. When I win I shall have my house back.'

'There's just one teeny-weeny little problem,' said Ratty.

'Really? What's that?'

'You can't drive.'

'Dear boy, don't be ridiculous,' said Mr Toad, one finger in the air. 'I'm the amazing daredevil Toad. I'm the finest of drivers the world ever knowed!'

'You went to prison for crashing cars,' said Mo.

'Piffle!' said Mr Toad. He paused. 'Where did you hear that?'

'It's on your Windipedia page.'

'Oh. Well, I suppose I did. But all that business was ages ago.'

'Wildwood have a racing stoat,' said Ratty. 'He's called Stiggy. He always wins.'

'What, even against the magnificent Toad?' said Mr Toad, hopefully.

'Definitely against you.'

Mr Toad's face fell.

'Well, I think Mr Toad's a really good driver,'

said Teejay. 'He goes very fast.'

'Exactly,' said Mr Toad, beaming. 'You're a young toad who knows her stuff. I'll show that racing stoat!'

He flung open the car door, got in, and tried to start it. The engine made a **SSSsCCRRRREEEeeeEEE** noise. Then it stopped.

'Did you mean that?' whispered Ratty. 'About him being a good driver.'

'No,' said Teejay. 'But there's a chance, isn't there?'

SSSsCCRReeeeeeeeeEEE.

Ratty shook his head. 'He'll crash on the first lap. Probably into everyone else.'

Mo blinked. Then he grabbed Ratty's shoulder. 'Of course! Rat, you're a genius. You've got it!'

'Have I?'

'Yes, you have! And it *is* it too.' Mo was nearly jumping up and down with excitement. 'The Chief Weasel said we could pick the race, didn't he?'

'How's that going to help?' said Teejay.

'I can't tell you,' said Mo. 'It might spoil things. But I know *just* the race to put him in.'

SSSsсCRReeeeeeevRRRRoom!

The car started. Mr Toad leant out of the window.

'Get in, get in!' he cried. 'I shall drive home fast to practise.'

'No thanks, I'll walk,' said Mo, quickly. 'But I'll tell Mr Ripton you chose the Four-Fifteen at Pipergate.'

'What a fine fellow you are!' said Mr Toad.

'What do you want us to do?' Ratty hissed to Mo.

'Make him think he's brilliant,' Mo whispered back. 'He's got to think he's the best driver ever.'

And Mo trotted off.

'He's a mole with a plan,' said Teejay, opening the door.

'His best plan was not getting back in the car,' Ratty grumbled. He put on his seatbelt. 'I wish *I* was walking.'

'All aboard?' called Mr Toad. 'Then away we go!'

Ms Badger's car shot backwards and spun around. It made a grinding noise then roared off, forwards. Mr Toad drove at top speed right down the middle of the road, honking at anyone who got in his way.

'See, Rat?' said Teejay loudly. 'Didn't I tell you that Mr Toad's a great driver?'

Mr Toad puffed up with pride. He started singing at the top of his voice.

'*Ratty and Mo say that driving is hard,*
But everyone knows that old Toady's a card.
Teejay can see who will win at the race:
The weasels are jokers, and Toady's the ace!
Poop-poop!'

'We're in big, big trouble,' Ratty hissed.

Teejay nodded. 'Whatever Mo's planning, it had better be *really* good.'

Chapter 13

A Day at the Races

The loudspeakers crackled. 'And now it's the event you've all been waiting for, the highlight of the day: it's the legendary Four-Fifteen at Pipergate! Ten laps of our track, and the fastest wins. So, ladies and gentlemen, take your places at the stands.'

The crowd's cheer was loud even down by the track.

'This is it,' said Teejay. 'Are you ready, Mr T?'

'Just a moment.' Mr Toad put on his driving helmet and goggles. 'How do I look?'

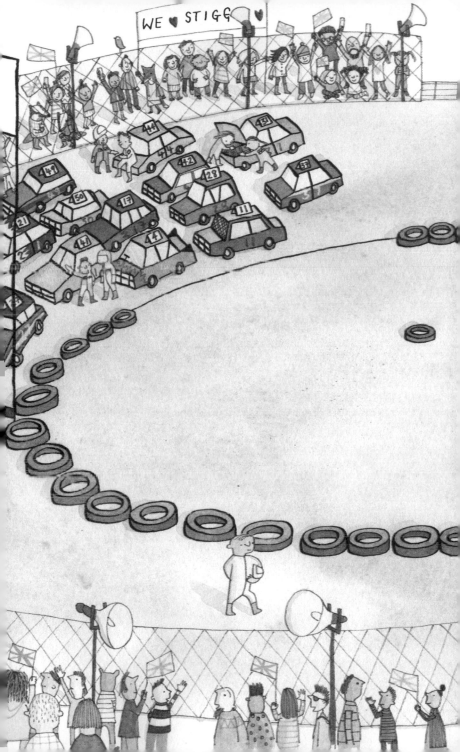

WE ♥ STIGG

'Not even slightly silly.'

'Did all these people really come just to see me?'

'Oh, yes,' Teejay lied. 'They heard that the best driver in the universe is here.'

'Well, perhaps not the *whole* universe,' said Mr Toad, humbly. He put on his gloves. 'Righty-ho! Let us give my public what they want.'

'Here they come!' shouted the loudspeakers. The crowd clapped as the drivers walked out, with Mr Toad in the lead.

He raised his arms and shouted, '**Poop-poop!**'

'What's that green thing?' called someone from the crowd.

'Dunno,' said another. 'Looks like a frog in a funny hat.'

'Is it a frog or a toad?'

'Either way it'll be a ribbetting race.'

Teejay winced, hoping Mr Toad had not heard. But he was busy posing. The last driver to walk out got the biggest cheer. He wore white overalls. His crash-helmet was white, with blue glass that hid his face. He went straight towards his sports car.

'Who's that chap?' said Mr Toad.

'That's Stiggy,' said Teejay. 'He's the stoat you have to beat.'

'Why's he wearing that silly costume?'

Teejay glanced at Mr Toad's helmet and goggles. 'Come on, let's find your car.'

Ms Badger's car was at the starting line in the middle of the others. They were all rusty and bashed-up. All except for Stiggy's, which was sleek and fast-looking.

'Drivers to your cars! Drivers to your cars!' cried the announcer. 'The Four-Fifteen will start in two minutes.'

Mr Toad climbed in. He started to sing.

'He sits in his car, the boldest of Toads,
In a race with the weasels
to win back his home.
The day is upon us when Toady must shine,
The weasels are stinkers,
Toad Hall will be mine!'

He grinned at Teejay. 'What do you think?'

'Very nice,' said Teejay. 'But I'd better go. Good luck!'

She shut his door and ran up into the crowd. She pushed through the people until she found Mo and Ratty, right at the front.

'How's Mr Toad?' said Mo.

'He's singing, so I think he's ready.' She

leaned over the railing. 'Ooh, you've got a really good view.'

'Yeah,' said Ratty, 'we can watch him lose his house from here.'

'Don't worry,' said Mo. 'He'll be fine.'

'But what about Stiggy?' said Teejay. 'His car looks really fast. He'll be finished before Mr Toad even starts.'

'Oh, I do hope so,' said a voice. Teejay spun to face the Chief Weasel, with Mr Ripton at his shoulder. 'We had that car built specially. It was rather expensive, but it does go very, very fast. Do you think that Mr Toad can beat us, Mr Ripton?'

Mr Ripton shook his head.

'No. Neither do I,' smirked the Chief Weasel. 'But do try to enjoy the race, children. I know *I* will. **Hurk hurk**.'

'What a nasty person,' said Teejay as the weasels walked off.

'But he's right,' said Ratty. 'Mr Toad can't win.'

Mo just shook his head, and smiled.

'Are you going to tell us what's going on?' Teejay demanded.

'Not yet,' said Mo.

'Ladies and gentlemen,' shouted the announcer. 'The cars are on the line. The drivers are ready. And that can mean only one thing—the Four-Fifteen at Pipergate has dawned!'

Chapter 14
The Race is On (Sort of)

Engines roared at the starting line. The drivers waited. Stiggy stared straight ahead. Mr Toad was hunched over his steering wheel.

Teejay glanced at Ratty and Mo. 'This is it. It's a race for Toad Hall.'

'All together now!' shouted the loudspeakers. 'Three!'

'Two!' shouted the crowd. 'One!'

'Go, go, go!'

And the cars shot forwards, horns beeping and wheels spinning . . .

. . . all except for Mr Toad's, which stayed

right where it was. The other drivers sped away, with Stiggy in the lead. But Mr Toad did not budge.

SSSsCCRREEEEEEeeeEEE went his car.

'Oh dear,' said the loudspeaker. 'Somebody give him a push!'

SSSsCCRREEEEEEeeeEEE

'Let's go down and help,' said Teejay.

SSSsCCRREEEEeeeeeVRRRRooM! And Mr Toad whizzed off the starting line.

Teejay's mouth fell open. 'Oh,' she said.

'I'm not an expert,' said Ratty, slowly, 'but I don't think that's good.'

'At least he's going,' said Mo.

'Mo, are you feeling all right?' said Teejay. 'He's going *backwards*.'

'I've never seen this before,' shouted the loudspeakers. 'He's facing the right way, but driving the wrong way! Can he do a whole lap like that?'

People laughed and pointed as Mr Toad rushed backwards around the course. He veered around one corner, then another.

'This,' said Ratty, 'is a disaster.'

'Not yet,' said Mo. 'Not until the next bend.'

'What are you talking about?' Then Teejay saw what he meant. 'Oh no!'

Stiggy was almost halfway round the track. And so was Mr Toad, going the other way. They were racing towards the same corner, from two different directions.

'They're going to crash!' said Ratty.

But at the last instant Stiggy dodged. He scraped past, and zoomed off.

The next driver, though, smashed right into Mr Toad.

Crunch!

The crowd gasped at the mangled mess of metal. Another car skidded round the bend.

Bang!

Then another, and another joined the pile.

Kapow! Tinkle! Wallop!

'I can't look,' said Teejay. 'Is everyone OK?'

A pile of broken cars filled the track. Angry drivers got out and shouted at Mr Toad. Above them the crowd jeered.

'What a toad hog!'

'He'll be toad away!'

'I newt we shouldn't have let him race!'

Mr Toad ignored them all as he worked, trying to get his car moving.

'I told you this would happen,' said Ratty. 'He's smashed everyone up!'

'Not everyone. Stiggy's still going,' said Teejay, glumly. 'He's bound to win now.'

'Well, it looks like the race is over,' said the announcer. 'There's only one car left and . . . no! No, wait! What's this?'

With a horrible tearing noise Mr Toad's car broke free from the heap.

'He's away!' shouted Teejay.

'Well, most of him is,' said Mo.

Mr Toad sped off. But the bumper, roof, and sides of his car were gone.

'Ooh, Badge is going to go bonkers,' said Teejay. 'She only just had that fixed.'

'Never mind that,' said Ratty. 'Look at him go!'

Mr Toad's helmet straps streamed in the wind as he hurtled after Stiggy.

'It's a race, it's a race!' shouted the announcer. 'It's head to head and stoat to toad, but which of them will rule the road?'

Chapter 15
Ms Badger's Nasty Surprise

Stiggy was a lap ahead, but Mr Toad drove like a toad possessed. The track was littered with bits of car. Here a wheel, there a door. Stiggy slowed to steer around them. Mr Toad just battered them aside. His car was wrecked, but soon he was only half a lap behind.

'Come on Mr T,' yelled Teejay. 'You can do it!'

'He's gaining, he's gaining!' shouted Ratty.

Teejay grinned at him. But then she caught sight of Ms Badger, coming through the crowd.

'Oh no. She's going to kill us.'

'Hello, you three,' said Ms Badger. 'Sorry I'm late, but I couldn't find my car.'

She watched the track for a few moments.

'My goodness,' she said. 'Those two are going quickly. When does Mr Toad's race start?'

'Ah,' said Teejay. 'Well . . . um . . .'

'That *is* Mr Toad's race,' said Mo.

Ms Badger's eyebrows shot up. 'And he's racing in that? But it's completely smashed to bits! It's on its last legs, it's—'

She stopped. She stared at the race. Her paws clenched on the railing.

'That's my car, isn't it?' she said, quietly.

Teejay didn't dare speak. She nodded. Ms Badger's face darkened, dangerously.

'Ms Badger,' said Mo, quickly, 'can I tell you something?'

He whispered in her ear. She listened, then nodded.

'OK,' said Ms Badger. 'But if it doesn't work, you'll all be paying for this out of your pocket money. For fifty years. Understood?'

118

'Yes, Badge,' said Teejay.

'You'd better pray that he wins.' Then she sighed. 'All right. Let's support our toad.' Ms Badger leaned over the railing and yelled, 'Come on, Mr Toad!'

'What did you tell her?' Teejay whispered.

But Mo shook his head. 'Just watch.'

Stiggy swerved around a corner, Mr Toad mere inches behind. Stiggy's engine snarled. Mr Toad's howled and gurgled. His wheels wobbled. Steam poured from his bonnet.

Stiggy dodged a heap of metal. Mr Toad bashed it out of the way. He stamped on the pedal. The crowd roared as his car drew level.

'It's the final lap! They're neck and neck!' shouted the announcer.

Stiggy pulled ahead. Mr Toad went faster. Black smoke poured out behind him. Side by side they shot around a bend.

'They're past the last corner. The finish is ahead,' shouted the announcer. 'But look, look! The track is blocked!'

Teejay gasped. Ahead of the racers broken cars were piled on the track. There was just space to squeeze down the middle. But it was wide enough only for one car.

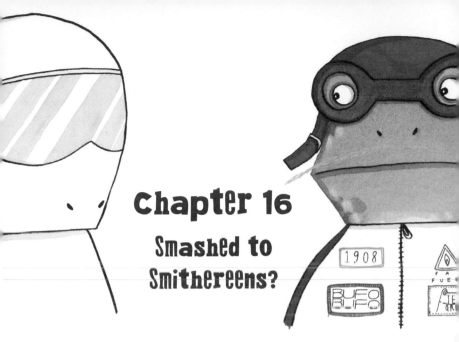

Chapter 16
Smashed to Smithereens?

Ratty's whiskers were stiff with worry. 'This could be bad.'

'Tell me when it's over,' squeaked Mo, peeking between his fingers.

Teejay grabbed the rail. 'Come on, Mr Toad,' she whispered.

The drivers bolted for the gap. Mr Toad turned to glare at Stiggy. Stiggy's helmet seemed to glare back.

'What a test of courage!' cried the announcer. 'Surely one of them must back down?'

But neither did. Faster and faster they went.

Closer and closer they drew.

'Do something, Mr Toad,' yelled Teejay. 'Do something!'

And Mr Toad raised a hand. He thumped the horn.

Poop-poop! Poop-poop!

'**Poop-poop!**' shouted Mr Toad. '**Poop-poop! Poopety, poopety-pooooooooop!**'

And he yanked the steering wheel.

The cars crunched together. They spun out of control. They slammed into the middle of the pile, and dust flew up, smothering everything.

'It's a crash, it's a crash!' cried the announcer. 'But I can't see what happened. Did they make it through? Have they both been smashed to smithereens?'

The crowd went quiet.

The track was silent.

And then . . .

Puttputt-puttputt-puttputtputt-puttputt-putt-putt-putt-

'I can hear something!' cried Teejay.

'So can I,' said Ratty. 'Someone's still going!'

A car wobbled out of the dust. It had no roof. It had no bumper. It had no doors or bonnet. It only had three wheels. It moved at a crawl. But behind the wheel was Mr Toad. His helmet was wonky and his goggles were broken. His face was covered with dirt. But his eyes were fixed on the finishing line.

The
 crowd
  roared
   him
    on.

**Putt-putt-putt-putt-
putt-**

Behind him the dust cleared. It revealed Stiggy, sitting on his bottom in the middle of the track, still holding his steering wheel. But that was all that was left of his sports car.

The rest was in bits around him.

'Oh, poop,' said Stiggy.

The crowd were on their feet. People shouted and cheered.

Putt-putt-putt-putt-putt-

Ms Badger was jumping up and down. Ratty was shaking with relief. Mo quietly smiled to himself.

'That's it, that's it!' Teejay shouted. 'You're nearly there.'

**Putt-putt-pu-pu-
pu-pu-p-p-p-**

'You've done it,' yelled Teejay, 'you've done it, you've—

'Oh. You haven't done it.'

The car gave up. It blew steam into the air. Its wheels fell off. Oil poured all over the ground.

'No, no, no!' Mr Toad jumped out. 'Not here, not here!' he cried. 'I was so close. Please, just a little further. Please, for pity's sake!'

He ran behind the car and tried to push it. He strained and shoved, but it would go no further.

Mr Toad sat down in the road. He shook his head. 'Oh please,' he said. 'Please.'

'He didn't finish.' Teejay stared at Mr Toad's car, just inches from the line. 'He didn't win.' She exchanged a horrified look with Ratty. 'He's lost Toad Hall!'

But Mo's eyes were glinting. 'What do you think?' he said to Ms Badger. 'Should I tell them, or will you?'

Chapter 17

All Legal

Teejay sprinted down to the track, with Ratty, Mo, and Ms Badger right behind. Mr Toad was still sitting there, legs out in front of him. He looked up.

'I haven't won,' he said in a small voice. 'Oh, sorry Toad that I am, I haven't won.'

'Don't worry,' said Teejay, 'I—'

'I've been such a silly, prideful old fool,' Mr Toad sniffed. 'My poor Toad Hall will be stuffed full of weasels by nightfall. They'll tear it all down!'

He pulled out an oily handkerchief and

blew his nose.

'Mr Toad, I think—'

'Thank you, thank you, but don't try to comfort me.' Mr Toad held up a hand. 'I've been terribly silly. I see it now. You tried to tell me, but I wouldn't listen.'

'You're not listening now, either,' said Ratty.

'My fate is sealed,' Mr Toad continued. 'A homeless Toad am I.'

'No, Mr Toad,' said Mo. 'We've—'

'You're kind, really you are.' Mr Toad raised his head. 'But I cannot stay here to be a burden to you. It's the open road for me, and the life of a travelling toad.' He pointed a finger up to the sky. 'Nights under the stars, eating with

the poor folk. That's the way for me now. Toad Hall has gone, and so must I.'

With a crunch of wheels a long, black car rolled to a stop beside Teejay. The Chief Weasel got out, followed by Mr Ripton. He grinned down at Mr Toad.

'Oh dear. Mr Toad's not looking happy, is he Mr Ripton?'

Mr Toad got to his feet. 'Unhappy I may be,' he said, 'but I still have my pride. I face you as a gentleman.'

'That's good, **hurk hurk**,' sniggered the Chief Weasel. 'Because we had a gentleman's bet. Remember that, Mr Ripton?'

Mr Ripton nodded.

'What was it again? If Mr Toad wins he gets Toad Hall?'

Mr Ripton nodded.

'But Mr Toad didn't finish, did he Mr Ripton?'

Mr Ripton shook his head.

The Chief Weasel's voice became a hiss.

'And that means that he didn't win. Doesn't it, Mr Ripton?'

Mr Ripton opened his briefcase. He pulled out a sheet of paper and a pen.

The Chief Weasel lit a cigar. 'Here's the paper that says you lost, and that Toad Hall belongs to me.' He blew smoke into the air. 'Sign it, Mr Toad. You might be a gentleman, but I like things signed. All legal.'

Mr Ripton held out the pen. Mr Toad looked down at it. And then, with a sigh, he took it.

'Goodbye, dear Toad Hall,' whispered Mr Toad. 'Oh, adieu, my beautiful home.'

He raised the pen to the paper.

Chapter 18
Poop-Poop!

The loudspeakers crackled. 'Ladies and gentlemen, your attention please. We are proud to announce the winner of the Pipergate Four-Fifteen Smash 'n' Dash Race.'

Mr Toad stopped dead. The Chief Weasel's head whipped around.

'How can there be a winner?' he roared. 'Nobody finished!'

'It was the bravest of contests,' shouted the announcer. 'But only one could be the victor. So let's go wild for our most *smashing* champion. He's the meanest and greenest, but not quite the leanest. He is the fastest of them all! He's the last toad standing! He's Toad of Toad Hall!'

Whooping and yelling, cheering and shouting rang from all sides.

'Mr Toad is the winner!'

Mr Toad blinked. 'B-but I didn't finish.'

'That's right,' shouted the Chief Weasel. 'He didn't finish!'

'He didn't need to,' said Mo. 'You should have checked the rules.'

'What rules?' roared the Chief. 'It's a motor race, ten laps of the track!'

'But Mo didn't enter them for an *ordinary* motor race,' said Ms Badger. 'The Four-Fifteen's a *banger race!*'

'And Mr Toad won because he broke everyone else's car,' said Teejay.

'Just the thing for a terrible driver like him.' Ms Badger grinned. Then she frowned at the Chief Weasel. 'And now give Mr Toad his house back!'

The Chief Weasel glared at Mr Ripton. The legal weasel quietly took the paper from Mr Toad and put it back in his briefcase. Then he pulled out a different sheet and handed it over.

'It says I won.' Mr Toad held the paper to his chest. 'It says that my home is mine again. Oh, happy days, I'm Toad of Toad Hall!' He smiled at the Chief Weasel. 'And look, there's even a place for you to sign. All legal.'

The Chief Weasel chewed through the end of his cigar in fury. But he picked up his pen and signed.

'There. Enjoy it while you can,' he growled. 'We'll be back for your home, Toady. Wildwood Industrious never sleeps!'

'Really?' said Mr Toad. 'You must be jolly tired.'

The Chief Weasel snarled. He got back in his car and slammed the door. Mr Ripton nodded to Mo, then got in too.

As the weasels drove away, Mr Toad took Teejay's hand on one side and Mo's and Ratty's

on the other. He raised their arms up to the cheering crowd.

'What do you say, young mole?' said Mr Toad. 'How about a "**Poop-poop**"?'

Teejay grinned. 'Go on, Mo. You deserve it.'

And Mo raised his chin and shouted as loudly as he could.

'**Poop-poop!**' he cried. '**Poop-poop!**'

Chapter 19

Why Ever would Anybody want to Drive?

M^s Badger turned into the grounds of Toad Hall. Teejay could see teams of builders hammering and sawing all over the house.

'Wowsers. Mr Toad's been busy,' said Ratty.

'But it still needs a lot of work,' said Mo.

'Good,' said Ms Badger. 'Hopefully that'll keep him out of trouble.'

Ms Badger stopped the car and Teejay jumped out. She ran up and gave Mr Toad a hug.

'It's looking great!' she said. 'Where did you find the money?'

Mr Toad winked. 'Oh, I have my sources.' He turned to Ms Badger. 'Dear lady, I do hope that you like your new motor car?'

The car that Mr Toad had bought her was huge and full of gadgets. Ms Badger said she didn't like it, but Teejay knew she did, really.

'Humph,' said Ms Badger. 'I preferred the old one. But thank you.'

'It was the very least I could do.' Mr Toad ran his hands over its paint. 'You know, I wouldn't mind one of these myself.'

'Here we go again,' Ratty muttered.

'Absolutely not,' said Ms Badger, horrified. 'Under no circumstances are you ever to get behind another wheel.'

'My dear lady—'

'Don't you "my dear lady" me. If it wasn't for Mo you wouldn't have a house and I wouldn't have a car.' She scowled. 'So you promise me, right now: no more driving.'

'Surely you're not serious?'

Ms Badger folded her arms.

'She's serious,' said Mo.

Mr Toad gave her his very best smile. 'Ah, I understand. You mean that I shouldn't drive every day. Just on a Sunday, perhaps?'

His face was filled with hope. Ms Badger's jaw set.

'No, I mean never. Promise me!'

Mr Toad looked from Ms Badger back to Teejay.

'I'm sorry, Mr T,' said Teejay, 'but Badge is right. You are a pretty awful driver.'

Mr Toad sighed and hung his head.

'Of course, of course,' he said. 'If you ask it, then so it must be. I owe you all such a terrible debt, it would be churlish to refuse.' He raised his eyes to the sky. 'So it's goodbye to driving and farewell motor cars. Henceforth, a pedestrian Toad. I have given my word.'

An aeroplane flew over, high above Toad Hall. It whisked from view, leaving a fluffy, white trail. Mr Toad's mouth dropped open.

'Besides,' he gasped, 'why ever would anybody want to drive? Not when they could *fly!*'

The End
(But not the End of the Toad)

The Wind in the Willows

The River Thames

Kenneth Grahame is the author of *The Wind in the Willows,* the book which has introduced generations of children to Mr Toad and his friends. Kenneth Grahame was born in 1859 and spent much of his childhood exploring the idyllic countryside along the banks of the River Thames and discovering its wildlife.

A water vole

Kenneth Grahame

After leaving school he began a career in the Bank of England. He married Elspeth Thomson in 1899 and they had a son, Alastair. When Alastair was about four years old,

(Left to right) Mr Badger, Mole, Toad, Ratty

The Bank of England

Kenneth Grahame began telling him bedtime stories that were to form the beginnings of *The Wind in the Willows*. The book was published in 1908 and has been loved by readers ever since.

TOM MOORHOUSE

When Tom was born, *The Wind in the Willows* was already nearly 70 years old. It seems to have always just been there, a normal part  of life. Everybody loves Mr Toad, Ratty, Moly, and gruff old Badger—and their adventures together on the river, the road, and in the scary Wild Wood. Tom never, ever thought he would get the chance to write more of these stories. If he's honest it's just a teeny bit scary. (He has an escape plan for if it goes wrong, quite possibly involving a washerwoman's outfit.) But he absolutely loved thinking up silly New Adventures for the irrepressible, irresponsible, sometimes irascible but never irredeemable Toad. And he hopes you'll enjoy reading them just as much!

Holly Swain

When Holly Swain was a small girl, she would sit under her dining room table and ask her mum what she should draw. She would happily draw the given topic until she had finished that picture and needed a new suggestion. Having developed a liking for a brief, she *knew* she wanted to be an illustrator!

Holly grew up in Canterbury and studied illustration at Bristol and Brighton where she still lives and works in a studio looking out into her garden and spending far too long watching squirrels eat her bird food!

If you'd like to read the original story, we have these editions available.